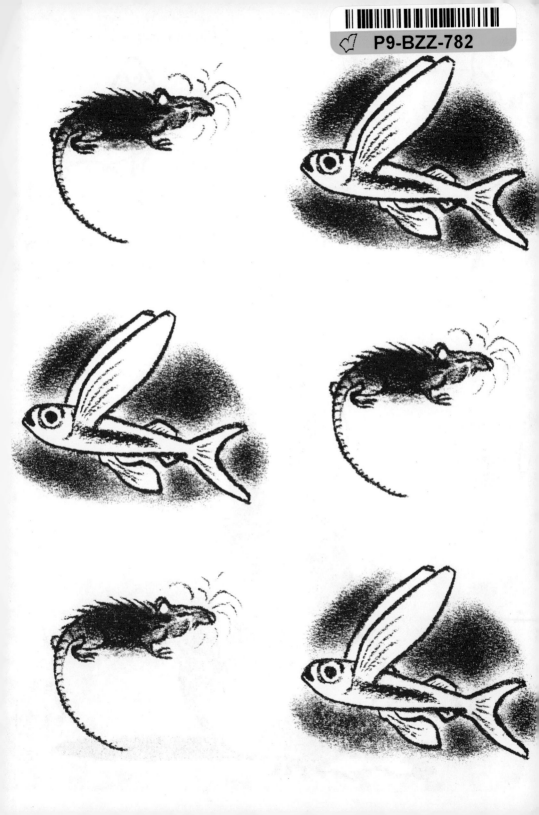

by
Jean Fritz

illustrated by
Marc Simont

Coward, McCann & Geoghegan, Inc.
New York

Second Edition, 1972
Text, Copyright 1954, by Jean Fritz.
Illustrations, Copyright 1954, by Marc Simont.
Library of Congress Catalog Card Number: 54–11356
Printed in the United States of America
04208
Weekly Reader Children's Book Club Edition

To David and Andrea

Fish Head was a cat. A raggedy, scraggledy, patched-up, scratched-up cat. And right to the tip of his chewed-up tail, Fish Head was *proud*.

Everyone on Clambake Island knew him. They were all used to seeing him pound down the waterfront with a stolen fish head dripping from his mouth. And so most of the people—most of the time—called him Fish Head.

But not the butcher at the Waterfront Market. He called him a LONG-TAILED LIVER-LOVING THIEF and he threw potatoes from the vegetable counter at him.

And not the people behind the waterfront windows. When Fish Head sat on the dock on moonlight nights and howled at the sky, they called him a Public Nuisance and a Dirty Wharf Cat. They threw empty milk bottles and old shoes and tin cans at him.

But Fish Head was quicker than the butcher. He was
quicker than the people behind the windows. He went
right on doing just what he liked to do,
        just when he liked to,
                and just how he liked to do it.
He was that kind of cat.

One drizzly Saturday night Fish Head was doing what he liked most of all to do. He was chasing a rat. A fat grandfather rat who knew the waterfront as well as Fish Head did.

In the back alleys they started. They raced through the shadows, flung themselves around corners, and skidded through doorways. Up fire escapes and over roof tops. Tail streaming and ears flattened, Fish Head was only two tail lengths behind when they reached the Waterfront Market.

Then—whish, poof! The rat disappeared. Right before Fish Head's eyes! Down through a private rat hole and into the Waterfront Market.

Fish Head slid to a short stop. He peeked down the rat hole and lashed his tail. His whiskers quivered.

He peered down the hole again.

Was the hole too small? Would he fit?

He measured it. It was as wide as his face, whisker to whisker.

Fish Head squeezed and flattened and stretched himself like a long roll of pulled-out dough. He wriggled and pushed and squirmed. Suddenly he found himself on the floor of the Waterfront Market behind a barrel of apple cider.

And there hanging over the side of the barrel was a long, drooping tail. On the other end of it was fat Grandfather Rat, panting and trembling.

Fish Head licked his lips and slicked out his whiskers. He crouched low. Slowly, carefully, paw by paw, Fish Head crept closer and closer to the barrel.

Grandfather Rat was puffing and twitching all over.

"Eee-eek!" he squealed as he smelled Danger.

He made a flying leap into a basket of grapefruit, with Fish Head hot behind him. Then up on the soup shelf! Two cans of split-pea soup crashed to the floor.

Up and down, around and around the Waterfront Market, Grandfather Rat twisted and turned, with Fish Head never even a shelf's distance away. Soap boxes toppled from their perch. Pickle jars rolled on the floor. Milk bottles fell and trickled on to flour sacks. A big bottle of treacle

shivered and broke into a thousand pieces as Fish Head
thundered past. Apples and oranges bounced into the sticky
pool of treacle. The Waterfront Market was upset from top
to bottom as Grandfather Rat reached his hole behind the
barrel of apple cider. Up he streaked and out into the night.

Up went Fish Head right after. Out onto the docks.
Over and under the wooden plankings.

Flop! Onto the deck of a boat.

Then Fish Head pounced! Front paws on a gray stringy
rat tail.

Blunderation!

It wasn't a rat tail at all! Only the stringy end of a rope
lying loose on the deck.

And Grandfather Rat was gone! He had slithered off
into hiding places that he knew best while Fish Head, who
had never been on a boat before, stood panting for breath,

not knowing which way to turn. Everywhere he nosed, there were strange new smells.

He looked in buckets. He looked behind a coil of rope. No Grandfather Rat.

At last Fish Head gave up and flung himself on the deck to rest.

He was still there when the funny chug-chugging started but he was too tired to notice.

Slap, slap, slap.

Sh-sh-sh-sh-sh-sh.

Putt-putt-putt. The boat was moving!

But not until the waterfront lights were just specks in the distance, did Fish Head look up. He raced to the deck's railing.

Where was the dock? Where was the market?

He paced the deck backward and forward. He climbed to the top of the mast. At last Fish Head knew that he was at sea, and he didn't like it! With an unhappy growl he curled up on an old piece of canvas sail and fell asleep.

All night long the deck became wetter and rockier. The wind blew tougher. The sea grew much, much rougher.

And Fish Head, a round bedraggled knot on a soaking deck, was more and more miserable. Finally he dragged himself dripping from the canvas and crept down the slippery deck towards a ladder and a patch of light below it.

He pushed through a door at the foot of the ladder and found himself blinking at a brightly lighted room, a tall red-headed sailor and a short bald-headed sailor.

The bald-headed sailor looked at Fish Head and nudged the red-headed sailor.

"Look there, Carrots," he said. "We've got a dratted stowaway aboard."

Carrots whistled a long, low whistle of surprise. "It's that sneaking wharf cat, Fish Head," he grinned.

Fish Head humped up his back and spat at the two sailors. He was that kind of cat. He did just what he liked to do.

At least he usually did. A sudden heave of the boat sent Fish Head sliding across the floor as if he had been on roller skates.

No sooner had he picked himself up than the boat tilted again. Head over heels he tumbled, bumping into chairs and banging against walls. He landed at the feet of Carrots, the red-headed sailor, along with a broken cup, two pillows and a can of tobacco.

Fish Head couldn't make his legs behave at all. Every time he went to take a step, the floor wasn't there. It was like walking on a see-saw.

And all the time, the two sailors were leaning back in their chairs, filling the cabin with great bellows of laughter.

"He's up!" Carrots shouted. "He's down! Flat on his nose!" He hooted and shook with his laughing.

Now Fish Head didn't mind being called names. He was used to milk bottles and tin cans and potatoes.

But laughing! No one had ever laughed at him before. And he didn't like it.

Fish Head loosened his claws.

He fumbled over to the sailor's chair.

Back he slipped. A few more steps.

Back again.

At last he hooked one paw around a chair leg.

Then out went the right paw, claws bared, on the sailor's ankle. A deep, clean swipe it was and well timed.

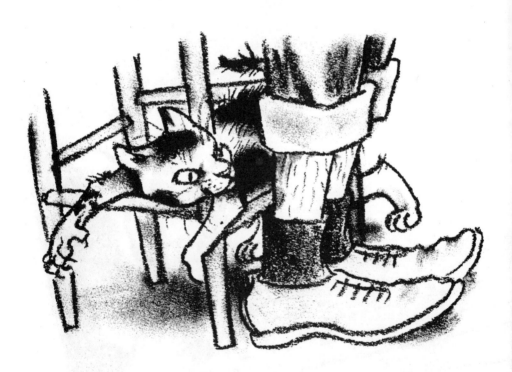

"Hot jumping frogs' legs!" yelled the red-headed sailor as he leaped to his feet. "You ugly spitfire, you!" he shouted at Fish Head. And he stood hopping on one foot, holding his other ankle in his hands.

Wham! Plop! Down crashed the red-headed sailor to the floor. Down crashed his chair on top of him. Down crashed a coffee pot and a plate of doughnuts.

For a moment it was very quiet. Fish Head braced himself. He got ready for the coffee pot to come sailing through the air. He crouched.

But Carrots didn't reach for the coffee pot. He didn't reach for anything. He just opened his mouth wide and let out a great, blustering laugh.

"Fish Head," he said, "you're a low-living, nasty-tempered beast. But I deserved that."

He sat up and rubbed his ankle. Then Carrots got to his feet and went to the ice box in the corner. He took out a chicken wing and tossed it to Fish Head.

Fish Head snatched the food because he was used to snatching food. But something was the matter. He couldn't eat it. His stomach felt lumpy and his head felt twirly.

For two days he lay quietly in a corner and didn't dare try out his legs. For two days the storm hammered at the boat.

On the third day the wind stopped. When Fish Head woke up, the sun was shining. The boat was bobbing pleasantly on the water like an apple at Halloween. Fish Head tried his legs and they worked! He could walk. He could even run. Quickly he padded across the room, out of the door, up the ladder, and on to the deck.

Water stretched away from all sides of the boat. But Fish Head didn't see it.

Three marshmallow clouds sprawled across the sky. Fish Head didn't see them either.

There was a clean, washed-up, fresh smell in the air. Fish Head certainly didn't smell that.

Because he was seeing something else and smelling something else, and he could hardly believe his luck.

There on the deck before him were three blue and silver fish. Lying there as nice as you please and ready for his breakfast.

Fish Head wasted no time. He had just sunk his teeth into the back of the first fish when something hard and wet came skimming through the air. It hit Fish Head plunk on the back. Whatever it was felt like a slithery cake of soap. It looked like a toy airplane. But it smelled like a fish.

And it was a fish. A flying fish with fins like wings. It flipped and flopped on the deck. Fish Head put a firm paw on it and saw that it was blue and silver like the others. It tasted like the others too—good!

When he had finished eating, there were four back-bones picked bare. Fish Head was lolling on the prow of the boat, taking a sunbath.

Every morning after that, at the first slit of daylight, Fish Head raced to the deck. One very exciting morning Fish Head found the deck slopping over with fish. He ate until his sides bulged and there were still five fish left over. After a while Fish Head could even catch fish in the air. He would spot one on the fly, leap up and land with it neatly in his mouth.

Fish Head learned many things. He discovered a tiny room with a steering wheel and another sailor. He was a burly, black-bearded sailor and they called him Kegs. Kegs and Carrots and the bald-headed sailor took turns at the steering wheel. Some days they turned off the motor and hoisted up a big white sail. Some days they dropped anchor instead. Then all three sailors stayed on deck. They took off their shirts and sang sailor songs so loud it set the buckets on the deck dancing. And Fish Head, in his favourite new perch in the crow's nest at the top of the mast, howled along with them. No one liked a hearty song better than Fish Head.

Sometimes they stopped at strange islands. Each time Carrots and the bald-headed sailor shaved carefully. All three sailors filled their pockets with jingly coins before they went ashore.

When they came back, their pockets were empty, but sometimes they carried fresh pineapple on their shoulders.

Sometimes they brought back baskets brimming over with chocolate bon-bons, peanut brittle, caramel drops, twisted licorice sticks, candied cherries, and figs.

One time they were all three blowing new harmonicas and wearing shiny gold rings.

And *always*, tucked away, there was a little package stuffed full of fresh catnip.

Fish Head never went ashore with the sailors. He wanted nothing to do with strange islands. He wanted only to set foot again upon the wooden plankings of his own dock on his own island. Each time he sighted land from his look-out point in the crow's nest, Fish Head hoped it would be Clambake Island.

Once it was Logman's Cove.

Once it was Biscuit Bay.

Other times it was other islands—shaped differently, smelling different.

One morning Fish Head saw again a round hump of land in the distance. Kegs was at the steering wheel while Carrots and the bald-headed sailor were shaving. The closer they came, the more familiar the land looked. It was certainly the shape of Clambake Island. It smelt right too.

It *was* Clambake Island! Fish Head could see the waterfront, the dock, and then the market. Now he could even
see the butcher walking up to the market with an apronful
of fresh clams.

Fish Head was the first one off the boat. He thought what fun it was going to be to rush between the butcher's legs and make him spill those clams. He pushed his hind legs up high. He levelled his head on the ground, ready for a fast take-off. But when Fish Head started to run, everything went wrong. His legs were wobbly. He stumbled. The wooden plankings of the dock seemed to be swaying up and down.

Fish Head was used to the roll of a boat. It took him all day to steady his legs enough to walk on dry land. By that time the Waterfront Market was closed and the butcher had gone to bed. And Fish Head was hungry. He saw a few rats scurrying around the dock. But they looked scrawny and uninteresting. Not worth a chase.

The moon came out and Fish Head stretched his neck
for a song. He yowled and wailed but it sounded queer.
His voice didn't have the good clear ring it had twenty
miles out at sea. Fish Head was restless. He was cross. He
didn't know what was wrong. The waterfront seemed all
at once a very dull place.

Then suddenly from the other end of the dock a deep
voice called out into the night. It was Carrots, the red-
headed sailor. He was standing on deck with his hands
cupped to his mouth.

"Fish Head!" he shouted. "Hey — Fish Head! All
aboard!" he called.

Fish Head stood up. He raised his tail straight up in the air as only a proud cat will do. Like a flag he carried it. And he swaggered over to the boat. Just as any sailor does who is going to sea. Fish Head jumped on deck as the motor started to chug.

Fish Head was doing just what he liked to do,
        just when he liked to,
                and just how he liked to do it.
He was that kind of cat.

About the Author

JEAN FRITZ was born in Hankow, China, where her father was a minister. She decided to be a writer at the age of five, and has since lived up to her determination to write stories about Americans. Her well-known works of historical fiction include *The Cabin Faced West, Brady, I, Adam,* and *Early Thunder.* Jean Fritz is also the author of several picture books for younger readers, of which *Fish Head* was the first, and has written stories for such magazines as *Seventeen, Redbook,* and *The New Yorker.*

Mrs. Fritz has two children and lives in Dobbs Ferry, New York.

About the Artist

MARC SIMONT was born in Paris but spent his early childhood in Barcelona. He studied art in Paris and New York and has worked as a painter and a teacher. He has also been a muralist for various buildings, among them the Library of Congress in Washington.

In 1957 Mr. Simont won the Caldecott Medal for his pictures in *A Tree Is Nice* by Janice May Udry. He has illustrated many books for children, including his own, *How Come Elephants?*

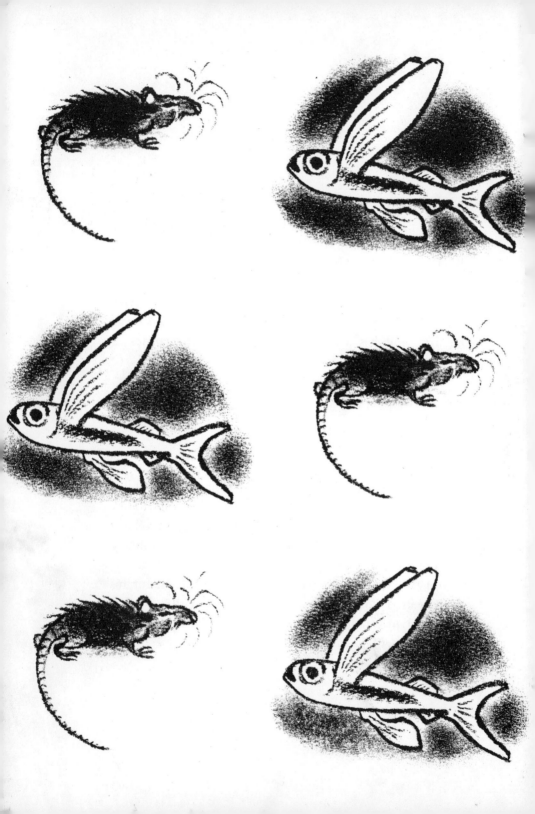